Fashion Fairy Princess

First published in the UK in 2014 by Scholastic Children's Books
An imprint of Scholastic Ltd
Euston House, 24 Eversholt Street
London, NW1 1DB, UK
Registered office: Westfield Road, Southam, Warwickshire, CV47 0RA
SCHOLASTIC and associated logos are trademarks and/or registered
trademarks of Scholastic Inc.

Text copyright © Scholastic Ltd, 2014
Cover copyright © Pixie Potts, Beehive Illustration Agency, 2014
Inside illustration copyright © David Shephard, The Bright Agency, 2014

The right of Poppy Collins to be identified as the author
of this work has been asserted by her.

ISBN 978 1407 13956 2

A CIP catalogue record for this book is available from the British Library.

Printed and bound by CPI Group (UK) Ltd, Croydon, CR0 4YY
Papers used by Scholastic Children's Books are made
from wood grown in sustainable forests.

1 3 5 7 9 10 8 6 4 2

This is a work of fiction. Names, characters, places,
incidents and dialogues are products of the author's imagination
or are used fictitiously. Any resemblance to actual people, living
or dead, events or locales is entirely coincidental.

www.scholastic.co.uk
www.fashionfairyprincess.com

Fashion Fairy Princess

Violet
in Jewel Forest

POPPY COLLINS

SCHOLASTIC

Dream
Mountain

Jewel Forest

Sparkle
City

Star
Valley

River
Sapphire

Shimmer Island

Glitter Ocean

Welcome to the world of the fashion fairy princesses! Join Violet and friends on their magical adventures in fairyland.

They can't wait to visit

Jewel Forest!

Can you?

Chapter 1

"Well, what do you think?" said Violet as she gave a little twirl in front of her three best friends. As she turned, tiny leaf-shaped beams of lilac light, reflected from the jewels on her skirt and danced around the wall of her fly-in wardrobe.

"Oh my fairyness! Violet, you look beautiful," said Bluebell, admiring her friend's reflection in the huge heart-shaped mirror.

"It was so kind of Primrose to send us these gorgeous gowns to wear to the ceremony. We would never have found anything like them in Sparkle City," said Buttercup. She gave a twirl too, and this time golden leaf-shaped beams of light danced across the wall.

The four fashion fairy princesses, Violet, Bluebell, Buttercup and Rosa, were very excited, as they had been invited to an important ceremony in Jewel Forest. Violet's friend Primrose was to be crowned Forest Fairy Princess in a special coronation at Tree Palace and afterwards there was going to be an extra-special party.

Primrose had sent each of the fairy princesses a sparkly gown with their invitations. The dresses were some of the most fabulous the fairies had ever seen, and they were certainly the most glittery. They had brilliant jewelled bodices and skirts that fell to the floor in soft folds of shimmering jewel-moth silk. What the fairies loved best about their gowns was that they were identical except for the colour. Violet's dress was a brilliant purple, Bluebell's a bright turquoise, Rosa's a soft pink and Buttercup's a shining yellow. They matched their wings perfectly.

"What accessories do you think we should wear with them?" asked Buttercup, tucking a wisp of her long blonde hair behind her ear.

"We must have something sparkly enough in here," said Bluebell, as she looked at all the open jewellery boxes scattered on Violet's dressing table. She fastened the clasp of a turquoise pendant around her neck and fluttered over to her friends to admire her reflection. Bluebell frowned. The necklace always went so well with her short, funky hair, but she couldn't help thinking that there was something missing.

"Why don't we try putting on our tiaras?" suggested Rosa. She smoothed her long, shiny dark hair and popped the glimmering crown on to her head.

Buttercup adjusted her own tiara and said, "These accessories would be perfect for a ball in Sparkle City, but the coronation is in Jewel Forest, where even the trees sparkle with pink and purple gemstones."

"Come on, fairies, we are the fashion fairy princesses of Glimmershine Palace,"

said Violet, smiling. "There is no way I'm going to let us be outshone by some trees."

"But Violet," said Buttercup, "these aren't just any trees. They are the wonderful, ancient homes of the forest fairies, as well as all the other magical creatures that live there. Our dresses glitter the way they do because they are covered in gemstones that grow on the trees' branches."

Buttercup was the most sensitive of the fashion fairy princesses. She could be very shy, but always found the courage to stand up for enchanted plants and animals.

Violet put her arm around Buttercup's shoulders. "You're right. It's just that I really want us to make a good impression. Primrose was so kind to invite us and to send us these incredible outfits. The least we can do is find the right accessories to go with them."

"There's nothing else for it," said Bluebell as she flopped on to Violet's four-poster bed. "We're going to have to go shopping."

"And I know just the place!" said Rosa, reaching for her pink silk handbag and pulling out a card marked with elegant, glowing letters.

Hazel's Dream Stones

Sparkle City's newest,
most exciting jewellery store.

Release your inner sparkle!

Diamond Boulevard, Sparkle City

"'Release your inner sparkle. . .'" said Violet, reading the glittery card over her friend's wings. "What in fairyland does that mean?"

"Well, there's only one way to find out," said Rosa excitedly. "Let's change out of our gowns and fly into town. If we need to buy something glittery, Diamond Boulevard is the place to find it!"

Chapter 2

"Look at those enormous sapphire earrings," whispered Bluebell. "They're the size of grapes."

"That's because they *are* grapes," said Buttercup, smiling. "They're the Jewel Forest grapes that grow on glitter-gem vines. I told you Jewel Forest was sparkly."

The four fashion fairy princesses had arrived at Diamond Boulevard and were

standing outside the crystal window of
Hazel's Dream Stones, admiring all the
glittering gemstones on display.

" 'Come inside to release your inner
sparkle'," said Rosa, reading from the
sign on the door. The sign had the same
elegant lettering as the card.

"Well, what are we waiting for?" said Violet, squeezing Rosa's arm excitedly and fluttering inside.

The magnificent window display had done nothing to prepare the fairies for what they saw inside. It was like walking into a giant jewellery box. Strings of glowing pearls hung from the walls like ivy, and the display cabinets were filled with every colour of gemstone imaginable.

In the centre of the shop was a glass counter piled high with necklaces, bangles, bracelets and crowns. A small fairy stood almost hidden behind it.

"Good morning," said the fairy, smiling at the princesses as they looked around the shop. "Can I help you?"

"We hope so," said Rosa. "Are you Hazel?"

"I am indeed," said the fairy, studying the fairy princess over her spectacles, which had huge diamonds, instead of glass, in the frames. "And who might you be?"

"My name is Rosa and these are my friends – Buttercup, Bluebell and Violet."

"My fairyness," said Hazel, "what an honour it is to have the fashion fairy princesses in my shop! Are you looking for something in particular?"

Rosa explained that they had been invited to a coronation in Jewel Forest and needed something fabulous to go with their gorgeous gowns.

"How exciting!" said Hazel, clapping her hands. "Please, take a look around and select anything you like."

She glanced over at Violet, who had been busily decorating Buttercup and Bluebell with strings of gemstones as though they were a pair of Christmas trees.

"I can see you have already found a few pieces," Hazel said, smiling at Buttercup and Bluebell, who were now so weighed down with jewels that they could barely flutter their wings. "But remember, there is no gemstone that shines as brightly as a fairy's inner sparkle. A fairy's inner sparkle can light up a room." She winked at the fairies through her crystal glasses.

"Yes," said Rosa, "We were wondering about your sign. What do you mean by 'inner sparkle'?"

"I thought you'd never ask!" Hazel said happily. "Finding a fairy's inner sparkle is my speciality. Now let me take a closer look at you all."

The four fairy princesses stood together as Hazel fluttered around them, studying them carefully. She muttered to herself as she made notes in a small, silvery notebook. After about a minute, Hazel snapped shut her notebook and rushed through a jewel-beaded curtain at the back of the shop. When she came out, she was carrying four velvet boxes, which she laid on the counter, one in front of each fairy princess.

"There," said Hazel, "try these."

Violet was the first to open the purple velvet box in front of her.

"A tiara?" said Violet, fingering the rather plain-looking crown. "It's lovely, but we already have tiaras of our own," she added apologetically.

"Aha!" said Hazel, smiling. "But these tiaras are special! They don't sparkle on the outside – they release a fairy's sparkle from the inside. Place it on your head and see for yourself. If I've done my calculations right, you will soon understand what I mean."

Violet tucked her curly dark hair behind her ears, raised the tiara and placed it gently on her head. As she did so the tiara began to glow with a soft purple light. Buttercup, Bluebell and Rosa watched with amazement as the glow grew brighter and brighter until they could barely look at Violet without covering their eyes.

"Wow!" said Bluebell, opening her box and placing her tiara on her head. As soon as she did so it began to release rays of intense blue light. Buttercup and Rosa were quick to try on theirs, and in moments Dream Stones was filled with a bright rainbow of light made from each of the fairy princesses' tiaras.

"These are perfect!" said Violet. "How can we ever repay you, Hazel?"

"It's my pleasure," said Hazel. "Please take the tiaras and anything else you like from my store and wear them to Primrose's coronation. If people ask you where you got them from, it would be an honour if you could mention my little shop."

The fairy princesses thanked Hazel and looked around for items to match their crowns. Violet selected an amethyst pendant and Bluebell the sapphire grape earrings from the window display. Rosa and Buttercup each chose glittering bracelets – Rosa's a pink diamond cuff and Buttercup's a gold bangle engraved with leaves.

Now that the princesses had put the finishing touches to their sparkly outfits, they had everything they needed to attend the Jewel Forest coronation.

"Let's go, fashion fairies," said Violet, grinning to her friends as they flew out of Hazel's shop. "The sooner we get back to the palace and pack up our gowns, the sooner we can fly to Jewel Forest!"

Chapter 3

"Wait!" called Bluebell to the fairy princesses, who were gathered outside her bedroom in Glimmershine Palace. "I think I forgot to pack my shoes for the coronation," she added, searching through her bulging rucksack.

"You're wearing them, Bluebell," giggled Rosa.

"Oh yes!" Bluebell grinned, looking

down at her tiny feet. "I couldn't fit anything else into my rucksack, so I decided to wear them on the way there."

The four friends were wearing their comfortable, everyday clothes for the journey. Their sparkly gowns and jewellery were safely tucked away in their rucksacks, ready to be taken out just before the coronation.

Rosa did one last check to make sure the fairy princesses had got everything, and then all four fairies zoomed down the palace's glass staircase, through the glittering oak doors, and out on to the cobbled driveway where the royal butterflies were waiting for them. The royal butterflies were the princesses' extra-special way of getting around. Jewel Forest wasn't far from Sparkle City, but the princesses had decided to save their wings for dancing at the party.

The princesses hopped delicately on to the backs of their butterflies, and with a beat of the butterflies' powerful wings, they began to rise above the sparkling rooftops of Sparkle City.

"Look, Bluebell!" said Violet, her long dark curls bouncing in the wind. "There's Sparkle City Academy. Doesn't it seem tiny?"

"And there's the mall," added Bluebell, pointing at the glittering glass dome that housed some of their favourite shops. "That looks big, even from up here."

As the fairies flew closer to the edge of Sparkle City, the buildings got further and further apart.

"We must be getting near," observed Rosa, pointing to the mass of glittering pink and purple trees in the distance. "Look!"

The fairy princesses fell silent as they began to pass over the jewel-covered treetops of Jewel Forest. Everywhere they looked, precious stones glittered in all the colours of the rainbow. The blossoms were made of gemstones, and the fruits, nuts and even the leaves glimmered and shone in the sunlight.

"Let's fly lower," Buttercup said, wanting to get closer. They had some beautiful plants in the palace gardens, but she had never seen anything quite like these.

"I think I can see a clearing up ahead," said Rosa, peering over her butterfly's wings. "Maybe we could stop for a moment and take a look. We've got a bit of time before the coronation."

The fashion fairy princesses landed their butterflies on the soft grass and set about exploring the clearing.

"What is that beautiful smell?" asked Rosa, breathing in deeply.

"I think it's these diamond daisies," said Bluebell, sniffing the sparkling yellow and white blooms in her hand.

"They're lovely, aren't they," said Buttercup. "Perhaps we could pick a bunch of them as a gift for Primrose."

"That's a great idea, Buttercup!" said
Rosa. "I'm sure she would love that."

The four princesses spread out in the
sunny clearing and began collecting the
diamond daisies. When their arms were
full, they returned to the butterflies and
laid their treasure in a neat pile.

They were all enjoying their break from
the journey when they were startled by a
shout from Violet.

"Oh my fairyness, princesses, look
what I've found!" she cried, holding up
a glittering green nut the size of her fist.

The fairy
princesses
crowded
round
Violet,
staring in
wonder at the
enormous gem.

"It looks like an
emerald nut," said
Buttercup.

"It's beautiful," breathed Bluebell, as
Violet gently placed the precious nut next
to the pile of diamond daisies. Then Violet
noticed a rustling in the trees out of the
corner of her eye.

"Hey!" she shouted, fluttering her
wings. "Shoo! Shoo, pesky creature! Don't
steal our nut!"

Buttercup spun round to see an

enormous fluffy pink tail scamper over to the nearest tree trunk and dart up it as quickly as it could.

"Oh, Violet!" cried Buttercup. "Look, you scared him off. He didn't mean any harm. Candy-tufted tree squirrels are just a bit cheeky, that's all."

"Didn't mean any harm?" said Violet, a little crossly. "He took our nut without asking. What's he doing now?" she added, as the fluffy pink squirrel dropped its stolen nut to the ground, hopped down next to it and started digging in the grass.

"He's burying it," said Buttercup. "The squirrels bury their nuts near their homes to store them for the winter. More often than not, though, they forget where they've buried them and the forgotten nuts sprout into brand new trees in the spring."

"Well, that's not his to bury," said

Violet, fluttering over to the squirrel and waving her arms in the air. The squirrel hastily pushed the nut into the little hole he had dug and scampered back up the tree trunk.

Violet picked up the nut and popped it in the pocket of her indigo denim shorts. "There," she said, smiling, "he won't forget *that* in a hurry."

Above their heads a loud chattering could be heard as the squirrel joined the rest of his friends.

"We'd better get going," said Rosa, eyeing the squirrels nervously. "I don't think it's far to the Tree Palace from here."

The princesses hopped back on to their butterflies, their arms filled with sweet-smelling daisies for their forest fairy friend. They were excited about seeing the Tree Palace for the very first time. Jewel Forest had already been such an exciting adventure.

Chapter 4

As the fairies approached the Tree Palace, the branches of the glittering pink and purple trees got closer and closer together, and it became harder for the butterflies to fly between them.

"This is silly," said Rosa, plucking a twig from her long, shiny dark hair. "Let's send the butterflies home and travel the rest of the way along the forest fairy skyway."

The forest fairy skyway was a network of delicate glittering bridges that connected all the houses, shops and palaces in Jewel Forest. The bridges were rebuilt by the forest fairies each spring from brand-new leaves.

"Good idea, Rosa," said Bluebell. "Look! There's a forest fairy decorating the bridge with fairy lights."

The princesses landed their butterflies carefully on the skyway. They thanked each of them with a kiss and sent them back to Glimmershine Palace with a gentle stroke of their silky wings.

"Hello there!" said the forest fairy, looking up from her tangled coil of fairy lights. "My name is Catkin. Are you here for the coronation?"

Catkin fluttered towards the fairy princesses, smiling broadly. She had

curly red hair tucked behind her pointy
forest-fairy ears and was wearing a
shimmery dress made out of ivy leaves.

"Yes, we are," said Violet, smiling. "My
name is Violet, and these are my friends
Rosa, Buttercup and Bluebell. Could
you point us in the direction of the Tree
Palace, please?"

"Of course. You just need to follow
the fairy lights along this skyway. I would
take you there myself but, as you can see,

I've got a lot more lights to hang." Catkin held up a long, tangled coil of twinkling fairy lights.

"Thank you," said Rosa, "I hope we'll see you later at the party."

"I'll be there," said Catkin, smiling warmly, "if I ever manage to finish untangling these fairy lights."

Violet and the fashion fairies hurried along the skyway, following the gently glowing fairy lights. As they fluttered ahead, they talked excitedly about seeing Primrose again and about the coronation.

"Look!" Buttercup gasped suddenly, pointing along the bridge of leaves. "The Tree Palace! Isn't it magical?"

Ahead of them stood the tall, broad trunk of an ancient pink diamond-nut tree. At first sight it looked like any normal tree, but as they drew closer the princesses

could see that it was actually a beautiful
polished-wood palace. It was covered
in magnificent jewels and had towers
that reached high up into the branches.
Drawbridges made of oak leaves and
spiders' silk connected the palace to the
forest fairy skyway.

At that moment, the drawbridges were filled with hundreds of beautifully dressed, excited forest fairies. They all had small, pointy ears, just like Catkin, and were wearing glittering outfits made of colourful leaves and jewel-moth silk. All the forest fairies were heading into the palace except for one, who was fluttering towards the fashion fairy princesses, waving.

"Hello, Violet!" shouted the young forest fairy with choppy nut-brown hair.

 She rushed at Violet and threw her slim, freckled arms around her. "You came!

Primrose will be so pleased. She sent me here to look out for you."

"Hello, Nutmeg," said Violet, grinning. "Princesses, this is Nutmeg, Primrose's little sister. Nutmeg, this is. . ."

"No! Let me guess," chimed Nutmeg, fluttering up and down with excitement and turning to Rosa. "This must be Rosa, in pink. My sister tells me that you're ever so clever."

"Thank you," said Rosa, laughing.

"And you must be Buttercup. Wearing yellow, of course," added Nutmeg to a startled Buttercup. "Primrose says that you're brilliant with animals and that you know all sorts about them."

Buttercup flushed pink and looked down at the leafy skyway beneath her feet.

"And that means you must be Bluebell," said Nutmeg, turning to a grinning

Bluebell. "Primrose says that you are the most fun in class."

"Thank you!" said Bluebell, laughing and putting her arm around the excited forest fairy. "It's very nice to meet you too. Do you think you could show us where we can get ready?"

"Of course!" Nutmeg said, taking Violet's hand and pulling her through the crowd. "You can change in my room. It's right

next to Primrose's. Follow me. I'll take you there now."

The four fashion fairy princesses and Nutmeg rushed over the main drawbridge and through the carved wooden palace doors.

As they stepped inside the palace, the fairy princesses couldn't help but gasp. None of them had ever been inside a tree before, never mind a tree palace, and it wasn't what they expected. The broad trunk of the tree was completely hollow so that a shaft of light shone from the top of the tree, right down to where they stood. All the rooms, hallways and staircases had been carved into the trunk, and the walls and ceilings were engraved with beautiful forest-fairy scenes.

"My fairyness!" said Violet, looking about her. "Nutmeg, the palace is beautiful. It must be so wonderful to live here."

"It is," said Nutmeg, flushing slightly,

but pleased that the fashion fairies liked her home. "It isn't usually this crowded, though," she added, pointing towards the sweeping staircase in front of them, which was filled with fairies. "It will take us ages to get past everyone." Nutmeg thought hard for a moment and then brightened. "I know, we'll take the secret staircase."

Nutmeg pulled the fairies into a little alcove away from the crowds of fluttering forest fairies. "I know it's here somewhere," she said, running her delicate fingers over what looked like a very solid wooden wall.

"Er . . . Nutmeg," said Violet, looking puzzled, "surely that's just a wall."

"It might *look* like an ordinary wall, but the trees in Jewel Forest aren't like the trees in Sparkle City. They are alive with magic and can hear us. Look . . . here it is," said Nutmeg, touching a pointy,

forest-fairy-ear-shaped knot in the wood.
"See? All I need to do now is tell it
where we need to go."

Nutmeg bent down and whispered
softly into the knot and then stood back.
As she did so, a wooden panel in the wall

seemed to slide to one side and then fold itself into a spiral staircase just big enough for Nutmeg and the princesses to climb.

Rosa, Bluebell, Buttercup and Violet stood speechless at what they had just seen.

Nutmeg, seeing that the princesses weren't following her, turned to them and said, smiling, "Come on, princesses, what are you waiting for?"

And with that, the five fairies rushed up the stairs and emerged into Nutmeg's beautiful circular bedroom. When the fairies turned round to take another look at the magic stairs, they had vanished back into the wall.

Violet was just about to ask where the stairs had disappeared to when she was distracted by a forest fairy sitting on Nutmeg's four-poster bed in the centre of the room. The fairy had glossy nut-brown

hair and was wearing a glittering green
gown. Her face was buried in Nutmeg's
leafy quilt. It was Primrose and she was
sobbing loudly.

Chapter 5

"Primrose, Primrose, what's wrong?" said Nutmeg, fluttering over to the bed and putting her arm around her sister. "Please don't cry. Look who I have with me. It's the fashion fairy princesses. See, they've come for your coronation! And they've brought you some diamond daisies – they're your favourite."

"Oh dear!" sobbed Primrose, crying

even louder when she saw the worried-looking fairy princesses standing at the end of the bed.

"Come on now, Primrose," said Violet softly, setting down the daisies. She pulled out a lilac silk handkerchief from her bag and sat down next to the crying forest fairy. "We can't understand you if you cry like that. Blow your nose and tell us what's wrong. I'm sure it's nothing we can't figure out together."

Thhhrrrppp! Primrose blew her nose loudly into the soft handkerchief. "I'm so sorry, princesses," she said in between sobs, "but I'm afraid there isn't going to be a coronation today."

"Of course there will be!" said Bluebell. "You look beautiful. All the guests are arriving. Everything is perfect. What could possibly be wrong?"

A large tear rolled down Primrose's delicate nose as she lowered her eyes. "You're right. Everything is perfect," she whispered. "All of the forest fairies have worked so hard and been so kind, and I've let everyone down. You see, there can't be a coronation because I've lost my crown."

"Is that all?" said Violet, relieved. "Well, you can borrow one of our tiaras. I know I packed a spare. In fact, I think it would go perfectly with your gown."

"That's very kind of you, Violet," said Primrose, "but this crown has been in the family for hundreds of years. It was made from the diamond nuts of the first tree ever to grow in Jewel Forest, and is filled with powerful magic. Without the crown, there simply can't be a coronation."

"I see," said Violet, "but it can't have gone far. Where did you last have it?"

Primrose led the fairies out of Nutmeg's room and into her bedroom next door. There she showed them to her dressing table, which stood by a large, leaf-shaped window looking out over the forest.

"I was sure I left it here," she said, pointing to the empty silk box on the dressing table. "I was polishing it to make it extra shiny, and then I set it back down and went to the Great Wood Hall for the rehearsal. When I came back a minute ago, it was gone."

"Well, let's have a good look for it,"
said Rosa, and the fashion fairy princesses
and Nutmeg set to work searching
Primrose's enormous bedroom. The room
was circular, just like Nutmeg's, but was
even larger and had more leaf-shaped
windows looking out over the glittering
forest.

"It's hopeless," said Primrose, climbing
out from under her bed after having

checked there for the third time. "I've looked everywhere. I think I need to go and tell Father to cancel—"

"Wait a minute, what was that noise?" said Violet, running quickly to the window.

"Violet!" said Rosa softly. "Primrose was speaking and we are her guests—"

"Shush," said Violet, putting her finger gently to her lips and then pointing out of Primrose's window.

This time everyone heard the familiar chattering sound coming from outside, and saw a fluffy candy-pink tail disappear into the dense leaves.

"I thought so. . . Primrose, I think I know what happened to your crown. It's been taken by the candy-tufted tree squirrels."

"They must have sneaked in through the window and grabbed it," Violet continued. "See, I told you we'd find it."

"But it isn't found," said Primrose sadly. "I still don't have my crown, and I'm still going to have to cancel the ceremony."

"Oh no you don't," said Violet. "We came to Jewel Forest to see you crowned a forest fairy princess, and we are not leaving until that happens."

"Violet's right," said Rosa, "and we're going to help." Buttercup and Bluebell nodded in agreement.

"It's decided then," said Violet, clapping her hands excitedly. "Primrose, how long do we have until the ceremony?"

Primrose looked across the room to the pink cuckoo clock hanging on her wall.

"About an hour," she said, frowning.

"That gives us plenty of time to head to the clearing where we first saw the squirrels, find the crown and fly back. Do you think you can hold off telling your father until then?" Violet said.

"I guess so," said Primrose, "if you really think you can do it?"

"Of course we can. We fairy princesses can achieve anything," said Bluebell, winking at Primrose. And with that, the fashion fairy princesses flew out of Primrose's window and into the darkening forest.

Chapter 6

The fairies flew quickly, following the leafy skyway and looking about them for anything they recognized.

"Thank fairyness for these fairy lights," said Bluebell, pointing at the twinkling lights hanging from the skyway's handrail. "It's much darker out here than I thought it would be."

"I hope we find the clearing soon so that

we can head back," said Rosa anxiously.

"Look over there!" said Buttercup.

"Where?" said Violet excitedly. "What? Can you see it?"

"No," Buttercup said hesitantly, "it's . . . just . . . I think I saw a jewel moth. They come out at dusk."

"A jewel moth," said Violet, laughing. "This isn't a nature walk, Buttercup."

"Wait, look down there," said Rosa, pointing to a bank of grass covered in diamond daisies. It had a big bare patch in the middle. "I think that must have been where we were picking daisies earlier."

As she spoke, the fairies heard a loud chattering behind them. They turned round just in time to see a pink squirrel scampering along the skyway, almost knocking them off their tiny feet.

"Let's follow it!" shouted Violet. "It could lead us to the rest of the squirrels."

With that, the four fashion fairies fluttered away from the fairy-lit skyway and after the squirrel, who was scampering further and further into the darkly glittering trees.

"Can you still see him, Violet?" asked Buttercup as the fairies approached the edge of the clearing.

"No," said Violet unhappily, "I can't see him anywhere. Can you, Buttercup?"

"No," answered Buttercup, "I think we might have lost him."

"Hold on a minute," said Bluebell, pointing to a nut tree at the edge of the clearing. "Did you see that?"

"What?" asked Rosa, struggling to see what her friend was looking at.

"I'm sure I just saw something disappear into that tree trunk," Bluebell answered, fluttering towards the tree.

"But that's impossible," said Rosa, puzzled.

"No, it isn't. Look," said Bluebell, gesturing towards a small door at the base of the trunk. "I think he went in here."

"Of course!" said Violet. "The squirrels must live inside the trees, just like the forest fairies."

"Can I help you?" said a high-pitched voice from behind them.

The four fairies spun round to see
a large squirrel standing with his arms
crossed, surrounded by more than twenty
of his fluffy pink friends. They didn't look
very happy.

"Ahem. Hello, squirrels." Violet cleared
her throat. "We are the fashion fairy
princesses from Sparkle City, and we have
come here to demand the return of forest
fairy Primrose's crown. We know one of

you took it and we would like you to give it back right now."

When she had finished her speech, the squirrels began chattering loudly and making angry gestures with their paws.

"I think you upset them, Violet," said Buttercup softly. "Tree squirrels are very sensitive creatures. Remember, we are in their home. How would you like it if someone came into the palace and demanded things from you?"

Violet's wings drooped. "You're right," she said in a small voice. "I can see I wouldn't like that very much. Maybe you could try talking to them, Buttercup? I just know they will listen to you."

Buttercup nodded and took a small step towards the squirrels. "Hello, squirrels," she said politely. "My name is Buttercup and I'm very sorry for the way my friend spoke to you. She really didn't mean it. She's just upset because her friend Primrose's crown has gone missing. I'm not sure if you know anything about it, but if you do, please could you help us?"

As Buttercup spoke, the squirrels quietened down and listened to her calm and soothing voice. When she had stopped talking, the squirrel they had chased along the skyway hopped forward.

"Nice to meet you, Buttercup," said the squirrel, holding out a fluffy pink paw for her to shake. "My name is Conker. I'm very sorry if we weren't very friendly, but we squirrels don't like to be chased, and this rude fairy –" Conker pointed to Violet "– chased me once already today, and took my nut. You, however, seem gentle and kind, so I will speak to the other squirrels and find out if any of them know anything about Primrose's crown. This is my house," he said, waving his paw at the nut tree in front of them. "Why don't we all go inside while I find out what happened?"

With that, Conker hopped forward and opened the little wooden door. He disappeared inside, closely followed by the four fairy princesses and the rest of the chattering squirrels.

"Wow!" said Buttercup, as she looked around the squirrel's tidy tree-trunk house. "You have a lovely home."

"Thank you," said Conker. "Please make yourselves comfortable." He pointed towards a little wooden table and four comfortable-looking chairs. "There is fresh beechnut tea in the teapot."

Buttercup, Bluebell and Violet sat down while Rosa poured tea into some wooden mugs. Conker was speaking to the chattering squirrels, whose fluffy tails jiggled and bobbed as they talked over each other excitedly.

Before long, he stepped forward to speak to the fairies again.

"Buttercup, I have talked to the squirrels and I am afraid your friend was right. One of us did take Primrose's crown. I will let Sycamore tell you the rest himself." Conker nodded towards a small, frightened squirrel.

"I am very sorry," Sycamore said, a tear rolling down his soft, fluffy cheek.

"I was upset that I hadn't been invited to the coronation, you see. Then when I saw the diamond-nut crown on the dressing table looking so shiny and lovely, I just couldn't resist it. I didn't realize that Primrose couldn't be crowned without it. She is my friend and I feel terrible. Come with me and I'll show you where I buried it, so that you can take it back to her."

"Oh, Sycamore," said Buttercup, "it is very brave of you to tell us what happened. I am sure Primrose meant to invite you! Let's go and get her crown, and then you must come along to the party as our guest, and friend."

Violet, Rosa, Buttercup and Bluebell flew after Sycamore as he raced through the glittering trees and then hopped down to the ground to look for where he had buried the crown. Once he found the spot, Sycamore dug up the crown and handed it to Violet.

"There you go," he said. "I'm glad I remembered where I buried it. We

squirrels can be a bit forgetful."

"Thank you, Sycamore," said Violet, "it
is a beautiful crown. I am sure Primrose
will be thrilled to have it back again."

"I do hope so," said Sycamore. "Well, I'd
better go and comb my tail for the party.
See you later." And with that, the fluffy
pink squirrel scampered off into the trees.

"We'd better get going too, Violet," said
Rosa, looking at the rose gold watch on
her wrist. "We haven't got much time."

"Great, now we just need to find our way back," said Bluebell, looking at the direction they had come from. "Um, princesses, does anyone remember how to get to the Tree Palace?"

Chapter 7

The fairy princesses looked at one
another in despair. They had found the
squirrels and got back the crown, but
now they were lost in the dark forest
with no way of finding their way back.

"What do we do now?" said Bluebell
anxiously. "I know we didn't follow
Sycamore far from the clearing, but we
zigzagged all over the place to get here."

"I think the best thing to do is wait here until Primrose sends someone out to look for us," said Rosa, looking around at the dark trees.

"But there's no way we can get back in time if we just sit here and wait for help," said Violet. "We can't let Primrose down. We have to at least try."

Rosa, Bluebell and Buttercup quickly glanced at one another and nodded.

"OK, Violet," said Rosa, "but let's go carefully, and let's walk. We will be much more likely to find our way on foot."

The fairies walked cautiously through the forest holding hands, taking care to avoid tripping over the tree roots. The night animals had started to come out and the fairies could hear strange noises that even Buttercup couldn't identify. It was so dark now that each fairy could barely see the fairy in front of her. Violet led the way, but she was in such a hurry that she stopped looking at her feet and tripped over a mound of earth.

"Violet, Violet, are you OK?" Buttercup cried, rushing to her friend.

"No!" sobbed Violet, staring at their surroundings. "Look where we are." Everything around her seemed very familiar, but not in a good way.

"I don't understand," said Buttercup,
helping Violet to her feet.

"Don't you recognize anything?" she
asked. "We're back where Sycamore dug
up Primrose's crown. We've been going
round in circles."

As Violet went to search for the bag she
had dropped when she fell, Rosa, Bluebell
and Buttercup talked together sadly. Violet
was right. Despite all their efforts, they were
back where they had started and were no

closer to finding their way to the Tree Palace.

"I really don't think we should carry on," said Rosa. "We could end up getting ourselves even more lost than we are now."

"You're right, Rosa. Let's find a sheltered spot to wait until morning," said Bluebell. "There are lots of soft leaves around. We could make hammocks."

"How about underneath that glitter-berry bush?" said Buttercup.

Rosa and Bluebell nodded and the three of them set about finding lots of soft leaves to make themselves comfortable hammocks.

Violet found her bag, and returned to her friends to help them set up for the night. She felt dreadful for leading the fairy princesses out into the forest, only for them to be lost in the dark. She opened her bag to see if she had anything to make the fairies' shelter more comfortable, and

as she rummaged, her hand caught hold of
a velvet box. It was such a shame that she
wouldn't get to wear her new tiara to the
coronation. She opened the box and in
the dim light of the moon she managed to
read the words printed inside the lid:

Release your inner sparkle!

"How could I have been so stupid?" said Violet to herself, but loud enough for the other fairies to hear.

"Don't blame yourself, Violet," said Rosa. "You just wanted to help your friend. You are very loyal and brave, and we would never call you stupid, even if your bravery does get us into a bit of trouble from time to time."

"No, but I *am* stupid," said Violet, clapping her hands together with excitement. "We *all* are! We've been carrying the answer to our problem around with us!"

"What do you mean?" asked Rosa, confused.

"Our inner sparkles!" said Violet. "All this time we've been looking for lights to guide us, when an even brighter light has been with us all along. Put on your tiaras – we don't have much time."

"Of course!" said Buttercup excitedly, reaching into her bag and taking out her tiara. Rosa and Bluebell quickly did the same.

The four fairies lifted up their tiaras and placed them gently on their heads.

In a fraction of a second the whole forest was filled with a beautiful rainbow of light made from the four different colours of the fairy friends' tiaras. The magical light was even brighter than daylight.

"Can anyone see anything they recognize?" asked Violet, squinting at the bright light.

"Over there," said Bluebell, pointing towards a beautiful emerald tree with ruby roses climbing up its twisted trunk. "I think there was a tree like that near the skyway."

The fairies headed towards the glittering tree. They were moving quickly now that they were able to see where they were going, and it wasn't long before Violet called out, "I've found it! I've found the skyway!"

Rosa, Buttercup and Bluebell fluttered towards their friend's happy voice and the four fairies raced along the leafy skyway as fast as their tiny wings could carry them.

"I just hope it's not too late," said Violet breathlessly. The fairies looked at one another in concern. They were relieved to be on their way back, but what if Primrose had already told the king to cancel the ceremony? There was no time to lose.

Chapter 8

"Where is everybody?" said Bluebell, out of breath, as the fairy princesses zoomed into the Tree Palace. Earlier in the day the sweeping staircase had been packed with excited forest fairies arriving for the coronation. Now the grand entrance was completely empty.

"They must be in the Great Wood Hall already," said Rosa, looking at her watch.

"The ceremony is supposed to start any minute now."

"But it can't start without the crown," said Bluebell worriedly.

"Quick," said Violet, pulling them into the little alcove, "in here!"

Violet ran her fingers over the wall to try and find the ear-shaped knot Nutmeg had shown them. When she found it, she bent down and whispered into it, "Take us to Primrose, please."

Once again the panel in the wall slid to the side and folded into a spiral staircase, just big enough for the fairies to climb. The fairies rushed up the stairs, which twisted and turned until the fairies fluttered out into a beautiful wood-panelled room with a high ceiling and jewel-glass windows. Violet thanked the staircase quickly before it vanished into

the wall, and was immediately greeted by an excited Nutmeg.

"You made it!" Nutmeg cried. "Look, Primrose, I told you they would come back safely."

"Thank fairyness you're all right," said Primrose. "It's so dark out there, I was scared that you had become lost or had fallen."

"We did both," said Violet, smiling at her fashion fairy friends. "But we found the squirrels and we made it back with your crown. I hope we're not too late."

Nutmeg and Primrose squealed with excitement and buried the fairies in hugs and kisses.

"You're just in time. I was about to go and tell Father everything," Primrose said, her eyes shining. "You must tell us what happened while you finish getting ready."

As the fairies slipped into their glittering gowns, Violet explained to Primrose what had happened and why Sycamore had stolen Primrose's crown.

"Poor Sycamore!" said Primrose. "He must have been so hurt that I hadn't invited him. I honestly meant to, but it must have just slipped my mind with all the other arrangements. Nutmeg, run outside and ask one of the fairy-flyers to hurry to the squirrels' home with a formal invitation."

"No problem," said Nutmeg. "Just make sure you don't start without me," she added as she fluttered out of the room.

"Violet," continued Primrose, "you've been so brave. I don't know how I will ever be able to repay you."

"It wasn't just me," said Violet. "I would never have had the courage to head out into the dark forest without my friends beside me."

Primrose nodded. "Thank you, fashion fairies. I am so grateful to each of you."

"And there's no need for you to repay us," said Rosa. "It was an honour to have been able to help you and be a part of your special day."

As Rosa spoke, beautiful music could be heard coming from the Great Wood Hall. The ceremony was about to begin.

"Well," said Primrose, smiling, "perhaps you wouldn't mind helping me one more time."

She fluttered to a tall wardrobe in the corner of the room and took out four magnificent jewelled cloaks. There was one in each of the fairy princesses' favourite colours.

"I was wondering if you would agree to wear these," said Primrose, handing a

cloak to each of the fairies, "and do me
the honour of standing with me during the
ceremony as my official fairies-in-waiting."

"Oh, Primrose!" said Violet, throwing
her arms around her friend. "Of course
we will!"

Violet, Buttercup, Rosa and Bluebell
fastened the cloaks' delicate clasps around

their shoulders and put on their tiaras, releasing a rainbow of light, just as Nutmeg slipped back into the room.

"Wow!" said Nutmeg. "Those are the most beautiful tiaras I've ever seen! Are you ready, Primrose?"

Primrose nodded and the four fairy princesses took their places behind Primrose and Nutmeg as they walked gracefully through the double doors and into the Great Wood Hall.

With the crown safely back where it belonged, the ceremony took place without a hitch. Violet, Rosa, Buttercup and Bluebell stood behind Primrose and her sister, and were thrilled to get a front-row view. They sang the forest fairies' sacred song, with a little help from Nutmeg, and cheered as the forest fairy king lowered the diamond-nut crown on

to his daughter's bowed head.

When it was over, an orchestra of forest fairies with beautifully carved wooden instruments played a bright and happy tune as glittering leaves fluttered down from the ceiling.

"You did it," whispered Violet to Primrose as they filed out of the hall. "You're a princess now. How do you feel?"

"Wonderful," answered Primrose, grinning from ear to ear. "I would never have managed it without you. You are such good friends."

"We princesses need to stick together," said Bluebell, giving Primrose's arm a friendly squeeze.

"Look!" said Buttercup, pointing at a timid-looking tree squirrel standing outside the hall. "I think that's Sycamore."

Primrose ran over to her squirrel friend and gave him a big hug. She knew that Sycamore was very sorry for having taken her crown and she was sorry herself for not remembering to invite him. Primrose took Sycamore's paw and the pair of them led the fairies out of the Great Wood Hall and out into Jewel Forest. The forest looked more magical than ever with twinkling

fairy lights and glow-worm lanterns
hanging from every branch of the glittering
trees. There were tables covered in silk
tablecloths and decorated with flowers.
Among the flowers sat carved wooden
plates piled high with forest fairy cakes
and jewelled fruit treats.

The celebration was one of the most fun parties the fashion fairy princesses had ever been to. Everyone admired their new tiaras and asked where they had got them from, and the fairy princesses told them about Hazel and her wonderful shop in Sparkle City.

As the fairies were dancing to the beautiful forest fairy music, Violet spotted the rest of the tree squirrels, with neatly combed tails, arriving for the party. She excused herself from her friends and went to speak to them.

"Hello, Conker," said Violet timidly. "I would like to apologize for chasing you earlier. Here." Violet held out the emerald nut she had found in the clearing.

"Thank you," said Conker, taking the nut. "You are clearly a very loyal friend," he said, smiling, "and one I would like to have for myself. Would you like to dance?"

"Oh yes, please!" said Violet, leading Conker over to the leafy dance floor. "We fairy princesses love to dance."

The fashion fairy princesses danced with the squirrels and the forest fairies until it was almost morning, when they fluttered back to Nutmeg's room in the Tree Palace. As they climbed into their silky leaf hammocks, a sleepy Nutmeg, who was so tired she could barely flutter into her own bed, yawned loudly and said, "I'm so glad you came. Please promise me you will come to my coronation when it's my turn."

The four fairy princesses smiled at one another.

"Of course we will!" said Violet. "As long as you promise not to let your crown out of your sight."

The fairy friends laughed together as they drifted off to sleep and dreamt of all of the exciting adventures they had shared in the glittering forest.

If you enjoyed this

Fashion Fairy Princess

book then why not visit our
magical new website!

- Explore the enchanted world of the fashion fairy princesses
- Find out which fairy princess you are
- Download sparkly screensavers
- Make your own tiara
- Colour in your own picture frame and much more!

fashionfairyprincess.com

Journey deeper into the world of
the fashion fairy princesses with more
exciting adventures!

Bluebell in Dream Mountain

Rosa in Sparkle City

Buttercup in Glitter Ocean

Fern in Star Valley

Honey in Shimmer Island

Use the stickers from these activity books to give
Violet a magical makeover on the following page.

And coming soon...